Contents

A Note from Tiffany Mandrake

Psst, this is me, Tiffany Mandrake, speaking to you from my cosy, creepy cottage in the grounds of Hags' Abademy of Badness. The Abademy is a place where bad fairies go to study how to be truly bad. It's not far from where you live, but you probably won't see it. The fairy-breed use special spells to make sure you don't.

It is run by three water hags, Maggie Nabbie, Auld Anni and Kirsty Breeks.

The hags started the Abademy because too many fairies were doing sweet deeds.

Sweet deeds are not always good deeds, and the world needs a bit of honest badness for balance. Otherwise, we humans get slack and lazy. The Abademy provides that balance. To enter the Abademy, young fairies must earn a Badge of Badness.

This is the story of Nanda Gemdibbler, a naughty gnome with an unusual way of being bad.

I don't come into this story at all, but the fox-fae told me about Nanda's naughty goings-on. I promised not to tell anyone . . . but you can keep a secret, can't you?

Sure you can.

So listen . . . And remember, not a word to anyone!

1. Nanda

'Nanda Gemdibbler! Have you ground
that polishing grit for Opal Trinket?'
said Gramma Glim. She popped out
of the passage connecting Grandpa's
workroom and the main crib with the
family dibble.★

★*Gnomes live in houses carved into the rock. These are called*
cribs. Each is connected to a dibble, or mine.

'I'll grind the grit later, Gramma,' said Nanda. 'I promised to plant pansies for Aunt Sparkle.'

'Gnomes don't plant things, Nanda,' said Gramma. 'They dibble for gems, then sell them to foolish fairies.'

'Aunt Sparkle plants things.'

'She should know better,' said Gramma. Then she sighed. 'All right, Nanda. Put on your apron and go to Aunt Sparkle's crib.★ Plant the pansies, then come and grind that grit.'

Nanda tied on her long apron and hurried out, banging the door.

'Glim?' Grandpa Clog peeped in from the tunnel. 'Where's my princess off to?'

★*Gnomes wear aprons for work. These protect their clothes and make the gnomes feel neat and tidy.*

'Nanda's gone to Aunt Sparkle's crib again,' said Gramma.

Grandpa sighed. 'I hoped she'd help polish some quartz for that young fairy Willow Gracecloud, but it's kind of her to help Sparkle.'*

Gramma ground the grit herself.

Nanda skipped along the rocky path towards Aunt Sparkle's crib. Unlike most gnomes, Aunt Sparkle had a garden. Nanda liked to sit among the flowers and play her fairy princess game.

Nanda stopped halfway between the two cribs, and slipped her hand into a space under a boulder. She drew out a sheet of polished silver and propped it against a rock.

---

*Quartz is a shiny rock that comes in different colours. Good fairies use it in magic spells.

She smiled.

Her reflection smiled back.

'I am Fairy Princess Alexandrite,' said Nanda. She twirled, admiring her curly fair hair. Green wings, like a cicada's, rose from her shoulders. Nanda curtsied to her reflection.

'Good day to you, lassie,' said a voice.★

Nanda spun around and spotted a tall

★*Bad fairies can wish others a good day. They mean, it's a good day for being bad.*

water hag dressed in faded tartan tatters.

'I need a wee bit of gnome magic, lassie,' said the hag.★

The hag opened her shawl to display a knobbly white ornament. 'You see my rabbit-bone necklace? A gnome called Clog Gemdibbler used special magic to mend the fastening.'

Nanda returned her looking-glass to its hiding place.

'The magic weakened,' continued the hag. 'I'd not like it if my bones fell apart, so I want you to restore it.' She lifted the necklace over her head and offered it to Nanda.

Nanda twiddled a curl. 'I can't do gnome magic.'

★*Each species of fairy-breed has its own magic. Gnomes work with rocks and metal.*

The hag grinned. 'Really?'

'I'm a fairy princess,' said Nanda. 'Can't you *see*?' She twirled, fluttering her wings.

'So,' said the hag, 'you won't help me wi' a bit of gnome magic?'

'I couldn't possibly,' said Nanda, sadly.

2. Nanda Gets an Invitation

When Nanda reached her aunt's crib, Sparkle was watering seedlings.

'You're too late to plant the pansies, Nanda,' she said. 'I gave up waiting.'

Nanda sniffled. 'I'm late because Gramma told me to grind polishing grit,' she wailed. 'Then I met a water hag with a horrible bone necklace!'

'That's Maggie Nabbie,' said her aunt.

'I hope you were polite, Nanda. It pays to be polite to bad fairies.'

'I'm a *good* fairy!' objected Nanda. 'Why should I bother with bad fairies?'

'Gnomes deal with all fairies, good or bad. Now, let's manure my roses.'

Nanda clapped her hand over her mouth. 'I just remembered! Grandpa Clog wants me to help him polish some quartz!'

That was true, but Nanda wasn't in a rush to help Grandpa. She wanted to play another princess game. Back at the big boulder, Nanda reached for her looking-glass. She tried to pull it out, but it was stuck. Nanda pulled, fluttering her wings with the effort. She was gasping when it finally came loose.

'That's the hardest work *you've* ever done, gnome girl,' said a smug voice.

Nanda stared about, but saw no one.
'Who's there?'

'I am, gnome girl.' A sharp snout
popped from under the boulder.

Nanda pouted. 'I'm not a gnome,'
she protested. 'I'm a fairy princess.'

'Nonsense.' The creature slipped from
its hiding place and posed in the shining
sunlight. Nanda stared at it. It looked like
a fox, but it was only the size of Nanda's
hand. It had a bushy tail and furry wings.
'Call yourself what you like,' it said,
'but I know better.'

Nanda pretended not to hear.
'I suppose you're an imp?' she said.

'I'm the fox-fae,' said the creature.
'A critter-fae, or fairy fetch.★

★*Critter-fae are imps with animal DNA. They are fairy breed.*
No two are the same.

I've brought you an invitation from Hags' Abademy of Badness.'

'What's that?'

The fox-fae curled its tail around its paws. 'Hags' Abademy is run by the water hags Maggie Nabbie, Auld Anni and Kirsty Breeks,' it explained. 'It's a school where young bad fairies learn Creative Badness. At the Abademy, you won't be lonely. You can be your real self.'

'My real self is a good fairy princess.'

The fox-fae cackled. '*Good* fairies don't get invitations from the hags.'

'They made a mistake,' said Nanda. 'I'm not lonely. I have friends.'

'Who?' asked the fox-fae.

Nanda considered. The other gnome girls she knew were pretty dull. 'Willow Gracecloud is my bestest friend,' she said,

pleased she'd remembered the name of
the fairy who'd ordered quartz from
Grandpa Clog. She'd never met Willow,
but she sounded lovely.

'Really?'

'Of course! We're both good fairies,'
said Nanda.

'Not according to Maggie Nabbie,'
said the fetch. 'Maggie was impressed
by your bad potential when she met
you this morning.'

Nanda giggled. 'That silly hag thought I could mend her bone necklace!'

'Read the invitation anyway,' said the fox-fae.

'All right. Where is it?'

'You're holding it,' the fox-fae said.

The only thing Nanda held was the looking-glass. Now she saw words appearing on its surface.

'*Are you a **naughty gnome?***' read Nanda aloud. '*Do you relish being **mendaciously misleading**, **very vain**, and **mindbogglingly bad**? Answer Yes or No.*' She giggled. 'How silly.'

'Is that a No?' asked the fox-fae.

'Yes.' Nanda read on. '*You are invited to apply for a Badge of Badness from the Hags' Abademy. To qualify, you must create and perform an original act of breathtaking badness. Answer I Will or I Won't.*'

Nanda looked up. 'Why would a good fairy want a Badge of Badness?'

'So, you'll turn down the invitation?'

'Of course I will.'

The writing changed again. '*The Hags' Abademy is a school where bad fairies learn to balance badness in the world. Go forth and be bad. The fox-fae will help you.*' Nanda looked up again. 'No,' she said.

'Too late,' said the fox-fae. 'You said *Yes* and *I will*. You accepted the invitation.'

'You tricked me!'

The fetch grinned. 'I'm part imp and part fox. Trickiness is in my blood. And now I'll help you win your Badge of Badness.'

'I can't go to a school for bad fairies!' protested Nanda. 'I'm too good!'

'Too bad,' said the fox-fae.

Nanda thrust the looking-glass into its hiding place and stamped her foot. 'I *won't* go to this Abademy. I *won't* win a Badge of Badness. Leave me alone!' she snapped, and ran home.

The fox-fae chuckled. Then it settled down to lick its paws.

3. Quartz for Willow Gracecloud

'Fold these aprons, Nanda,' Gramma Glim said as Nanda entered the crib.

'Sorry, Gramma, I can't.' Nanda reminded herself she was a *good* fairy. 'I promised to help Grandpa Clog polish the quartz.'

'He's finished,' said Gramma. 'So fold the aprons.'

'But Gramma . . .'

'*Now*, Nanda. I have to deliver that quartz to Willow Gracecloud at Catkin Cottage. I expect she needs it for some fairy spell or other.'

Nanda clasped her hands. 'You're visiting *Willow Gracecloud*? Oh, *Gramma*! Let *me* go for you!'

'Very well,' said Gramma. 'I have plenty to do here.'

Nanda gave a little twirl. Now she could show that fox-fae what a good fairy she was.

'Mind, Nanda, no silly games,' said Gramma. 'Go straight to Catkin Cottage, give the quartz to Willow and come straight back.'

Nanda skipped down the tunnel to the workroom where she found Grandpa Clog packing the quartz. 'I'm taking that quartz to Willow for Gramma,' she said.

Grandpa Clog smiled. 'That's sweet of you, Princess.' He handed Nanda the basket.

Nanda blew him a kiss. Then she went out through the dibble. As the mountain path wound down between rocks and scrub, Nanda hurried past other cribs and dibbles. She didn't want the tiresome gnome girls who lived there to see her and ask to come along.

The path levelled out and the forest began, and soon Nanda reached a valley.

She splashed her face and hands in a stream, dried them on her apron, and made a wildflower garland. Then she collected some pebbles. A dash of pebble magic made them shine. Next, Nanda added quartz and wove silver wire around the pebbles to make a necklace. Then she skipped off to Catkin Cottage, singing as she went.

The fox-fae popped out from behind a tree. 'Off to do a bad deed?'

Nanda frowned. 'I told you, I'm not interested in bad deeds or in schools for bad fairies. I'm taking this quartz to my friend Willow. Goodbye.' She skipped on.

The fox-fae was puzzled. Nanda Gemdibbler didn't *seem* like a bad fairy, but the hags never made mistakes. It decided to watch her closely.

4. Catkin Cottage

At Catkin Cottage, dainty cakes cooled
on Willow Gracecloud's windowsill.
Posies bloomed in crystal bowls. On a
pink cushion lay Willow's Seal of
Sweetness, earned when she was a pupil
at Miss Kisses' Academy.★

★*Good fairies who attend the Academy earn a badge called a*
Seal of Sweetness if they do enough good deeds.

And today Willow was going to see Miss Kisses again. She peeped out at the sundial. A gnome from the mountain village should be here soon with the polished quartz. Miss Kisses used quartz for *such* sweet spells.

Someone tapped on the door, and Willow flitted to open it. She blinked. The girl on the doorstep looked like a gnome, but she was taller than most gnomes. She had curly fair hair and large wings. Behind her slunk a strange fox-creature. Maybe it was an imp. Willow reached for the basket, but the girl hung on, peering into the cottage.

'I'll take that, thanks,' said Willow, tugging at the basket's handle.

'I'll carry it in for you.' The girl marched in with the imp-thing slinking behind her.

'Thank you,' said Willow. 'Do I know you?'

The girl laughed. 'Silly! I'm *Nanda*! You know that!' She glanced at the imp. 'Isn't Willow funny?'

Willow waited for Nanda to leave, but the gnome flopped into Willow's favourite pink velvet chair. Her gaze flickered towards the windowsill. 'What sweet fairy cakes.'

'I'd offer you some,' said Willow, 'but they're for Miss Kisses' party.'

'Dear Miss Kisses!' gushed the gnome.

'Do you know Miss Kisses?' Willow was surprised. 'I thought I knew everyone at the Academy.'

'The Academy?' asked the gnome.

'Miss Kisses' Academy of Sweetness for Little Fairies,' said Willow. 'It's where Miss Kisses teaches fairies sweet deeds.'

She sighed. 'I graduated three summers ago. I *do* miss the lovely times we had. Parties in the Pink Pavilion. Writing up our Sweet Deed Books in Daisy Dorm ...' She looked at the gnome girl in the chair. 'Do you know Miss Kisses well, Nanda?'

Nanda blinked rapidly, then smiled, showing large white teeth.*

'Of course,' she said. 'Miss Kisses will be my teacher at the Academy.'

Willow pictured the fairies at the Academy, in their puffy pink frocks. She couldn't imagine how Nanda would fit in.

*

Gnomes need strong teeth because grit from their dibbles gets into their food.

Nanda was delighted with Catkin
Cottage, and with Willow. Willow had
ringlets and wore a silken dress with kiss-
trimmed petticoats. Her wings glittered,
and her slippers had pink sparkles. There
was only one problem. Willow was going
to a party, and wanted Nanda to leave.

'Can't I stay a while?' wheedled
Nanda. 'I'm tired after carrying the
quartz all this way.'

'Just for a bit,' said Willow. She set an empty crystal jug on the table and flicked her wand, filling the jug with sparkling liquid.

'*Oooh!*' said Nanda.

Willow smiled. 'I store sugar-sip in the wishing well. I transported some to the jug.'

Nanda clasped her hands together in delight. 'I've never tasted sugar-sip! Gramma Glim says water is good enough for me.'

Actually, Gramma said her water was good enough for anyone, because the dibble spring it came from was the purest in the world, but Nanda didn't say that.

Willow looked surprised. 'Really?'

'I wish *I* could magic drinks from a well,' said Nanda as she drank her pink, fizzy sugar-sip.

'You will be able to soon,' said Willow kindly. 'Miss Kisses will teach you sweet spells when you go to the Academy.' She glanced at the sundial. 'I must go, Nanda. Miss Kisses needs this quartz for the Fairy Floral Fair tomorrow.' She reached for the basket, but Nanda picked it up again.

'I'll carry the quartz to the Academy,' said Nanda. 'It's too heavy for you, Willow dear.'

'Aren't you tired?' reminded Willow.

Nanda smiled. 'Your sugar-sip made me feel better.'

5. Miss Kisses' Academy for Little Fairies

Willow, Nanda and the fox-fae flew through the trees. Nanda bumbled and stumbled in the air.★ The quartz basket weighed her down.

She was exhausted by the time they left the forest.

★*Gnomes are heavy and their wings are small. They mostly fly low to the ground, looking for fresh supplies of quartz.*

'Why not walk?' asked the fox-fae, zooming close to Nanda's ear.

'Fairies fly,' panted Nanda. 'Leave me alone!' She beat her wings furiously, scattering a flock of bluebirds. The birds squawked at her.

'I'll help you,' said the fox-fae. It dived down to seize the basket handle in its teeth.

'I can carry it!' Nanda wobbled as she took the weight again.

'Fine!' The fox-fae settled comfortably on the quartz.

Nanda was about to tip the fox-fae off when she remembered she was a *good* fairy. At last, she saw Willow dropping lightly to the ground. Nanda tumbled beside her, and spilled herself, the fox-fae and the basket of quartz across a soft lawn.

They had landed in a garden, enclosed by a high brick wall. The bricks were painted sugar pink. Nanda blinked as she scrambled up. Everything seemed pink. The flowers were pink. So were the sweet little bird houses. The trees had pink blossoms. The grass was starred with pink daisies.

Nanda took a deep breath. It was lovely! It was sweet! It was pink! This was where she belonged! The smell of pink bubblegum hung over the garden, making her nose itch. Nanda sneezed. So did the fox-fae. It rubbed its sharp muzzle against the grass.

Willow picked up the spilt quartz and put it back in the basket. 'Thanks,' she said to Nanda. 'But you should go home now. Your grandmother will wonder where you are.'

'She knows I'm with you.' Nanda looked delightedly at the stone building that towered over the trees. 'Is that the school?'

'Yes. Isn't it splendid?' Willow smiled as a flock of fairies flitted out from the school. They wore puffy pink frocks with petticoats. They had pink slippers and sparkle-tipped wands. The leader had a pink brooch pinned to her frock.*

'Willow!' they squealed. 'Willow, Willow, *Willow*!'

'It's so *good* to see you!' cried the lead fairy, whose name was Fennel Featherflower.

'It's pink-party time,' said Flora Pine.

'The bluebirds said you were coming,' said Tansy Glitterwing.

---

*This was her Seal of Sweetness.

The fairies took Willow's hands, and towed her towards the open door.

Nanda followed, with the fox-fae at her heels.

'This is no place for you,' said the fox-fae, sneezing.

Nanda gazed hungrily at the pink curtains flapping gently at the windows. And there at the door was a tall fairy in a pink robe, silver slippers and a tiara.

'Willow dear!' exclaimed Miss Kisses.

'Miss Kisses!' Willow said, flitting

forward. 'I'm *so* happy to see you again!'

'Come in, dear.' Miss Kisses smiled. 'Fairies! Let's take Willow to the Pink Pavilion for the party!'

The little fairies crowded about, fluttering their wings and waving their wands. Between them, they swept Willow into the Academy. Nanda's nose bumped against the door as it closed.

She reached for the doorhandle, but it wasn't there.

'It's a Keep Out spell,' explained the fox-fae. 'That's how good fairies keep out uninvited guests.'

'I want to go to the party!' objected Nanda. She clasped her hands together. 'Isn't Miss Kisses *beautiful*? Did you see her darling slippers? Did you— *a-a-choo*!' She sneezed. The smell of pink bubblegum was overpowering.

The fox-fae sniffed about the door. 'You can't want to go in there,' it said. 'It stinks of sweet deeds. The smell makes my fangs ache.' Its muzzle quivered. 'This doorstep is stone. Gnome magic might get you past it.'

'I don't do gnome magic,' said Nanda. She banged on the door. 'Willow, let me in!'

'She's forgotten you,' said the fox-fae. 'And the others didn't notice you. They're only interested in *good* fairies.'

'She'll feel really upset when she remembers me,' said Nanda. 'I have to get in, and make her feel better.' She banged on the door again, then went to peer through the windows.

'Just like any bad fairy, you won't take no for an answer.' The fox-fae showed its fangs in a grin.

'I'm *not* a bad fairy!' grumbled Nanda.

'Of course you are.' The fox-fae buzzed to the next window. 'This is the Pink Pavilion,' it reported, when Nanda caught up. 'The party's started.'

Nanda flattened her nose against the glass. '*Ahhh,*' she moaned. 'They're eating fairy cakes, and drinking sugar-sip!' She hammered her fists on the window. 'Let me in!'

Inside the Pink Pavilion, Miss Kisses frowned prettily. 'Willow, dear, there's a gnome outside. Find out what she wants.'

Willow gasped. 'I quite forgot! That's Nanda!'

'Who's Nanda, dear?' asked Miss Kisses.

'Nanda Gemdibbler. She wants to come to the Academy.'

Miss Kisses tinkled a laugh. 'How cute!

We've never had a *gnome* here before.'

'Nanda wants to learn sweet deeds.'

'Then she must have her chance!'
Miss Kisses peeped out the window.
'What a pity, she's gone.'

But Nanda hadn't gone. She'd crawled
through a half-open window into a
dormitory.

The fox-fae leapt after her and sniffed
at the nearest pink bed. 'Try one,' it
suggested.

'*Oooh*, yes!' Nanda bounced onto the
bed. The springs twanged and broke.
The bed was made for fairies, not for
sturdy gnomes.

'Try another,' said the fox-fae,
grinning.

The next bed didn't break, but Nanda's
clogs smudged the pink satin quilt. She
jumped off the bed, knocking the pillow

to the floor. 'Look!' She bounced over to the dainty dressing table, and picked up a delicate pink comb. 'I'll tidy myself up.' She dragged the comb through her curls, breaking several of its teeth, then turned to admire her reflection.

'*Nooo!*' she exclaimed, staring into the fairy looking-glass. 'I'm a mess!' She dropped the glass, and turned away. 'I have to find Willow.' She opened the first door, but it didn't lead to the Pink Pavilion. Instead, it led to a bathroom. A pink tub stood in the middle of the room, and around it hung pink fluffy towels. Bottles of pink bubblebath lined the shelves. There was pink soap, and a fuzzy pink bathmat.

'Perfect!' said Nanda, and sneezed. 'I'll get clean before I join the party.' She turned on both taps at full blast.

Then she tipped three bottles of bubblebath into the bath. The air filled with scented steam, and bubbles piled up on the water.

Nanda kicked off her clogs, undid her apron, and removed her skirt and blouse. Then she stepped into the bath, and splashed down among the bubbles.

The fox-fae watched happily as water flooded across the floor.

Then it slunk out the window and flew away.

6. Nanda Gets a Job

'*Eeeeeek!*' Someone squealed in the dormitory.

Nanda had finished her bath, so she poked out her head to investigate.

'*Eeeeeek!*' Three fairies goggled at her.

'There's a *gnome* in the bathroom.'

'She's broken Snowdrop's *bed*!'

Nanda grinned. 'Hello! I'm Willow's best friend forever, Princess Alexandrite.'

The little fairies stared.

'You're not Willow's bestie,' said one.

'You're just a gnome,' said another.

'You made a horrid mess. Miss Kisses will be cross.'

Nanda laughed. 'You're teasing me! Willow is always talking about the fun you all have together. I'm coming here soon to learn about sweet deeds. I've begun already. I carried the quartz *all* the way here for Willow.'

The fairies weren't listening. They rushed out, so Nanda followed, still chattering. The party had finished, and Miss Kisses was talking to Willow in the Rainbow Room.

'I hope you'll look after the Academy Display at the Fairy Floral Fair,' she said. 'That way I won't have to leave the little fairies alone for two whole days.'

'I'd love to,' said Willow. 'But what about my flowers and the bluebirds and——'

She broke off as Nanda and the fairies rushed in.

'Miss Kisses! Miss Kisses!' chorussed the fairies.

Miss Kisses held up her hand. 'Go and write in your Sweet Deed Books, darlings. I'm talking to Willow.'

Obediently, the fairies fluttered out, and Miss Kisses turned back to Willow. 'I'm asking too much of you,' she said. 'Never mind, we won't have a display at the fair this year.'

'But we must!' said Willow. 'I suppose Catkin Cottage will be all right.'

'You could get someone to mind it,' said Miss Kisses. She turned to Nanda and raised her eyebrows. 'You must be little Nanda! Willow says you hope to come to us as a pupil?'

'Yes please!' squealed Nanda, fluttering her wings with glee.

'We'll have to see about it one day.'

Nanda twirled in a circle. 'I'll do *anything* if you let me come, Miss Kisses.

To prove it, I'll look after Willow's
cute cottage while she's away. Really,
I'd *love* to!'

'I can't put you to the trouble,' faltered
Willow.

Miss Kisses smiled. 'If this dear little
gnome wants to help out, everything's
settled.'

Willow offered her wand to Nanda.
'You'll need this to get inside the cottage,'
she said. 'But really, don't feel as if you
have to do this.'

Nanda hugged herself. 'I *want* to,' she
said. She smiled, and sniffled. The pink
bubblebath seemed to have soaked into
her skin. 'If a fairy can't depend on her
bestie for help, who can she depend on?'

Willow wasn't listening. 'You mustn't
touch my spells,' she continued. 'Really,
there's so little to do, there's no need to

stay in the cottage. Maybe you could just call in to feed the bluebirds.'

'Willow, it's *not* a problem,' said Nanda. She sneezed. 'Don't worry. I'll treat Catkin Cottage as if it was my own.'

Miss Kisses touched Willow's shoulder. 'Wonderful! Now Nanda can prove what a good, sweet gnome she is. Meanwhile, you can go to the fair.'

*

Nanda was overjoyed with her new job. When Miss Kisses saw what a good fairy she was, *surely* she'd invite her to come to the Academy immediately.

As Nanda left the Academy, she used Willow's wand to wave goodbye. A scatter of sparkles shot out, leaving a scorch mark on the wall and a smell like burning sugar. 'I'll be back!' she trilled, and skipped away.

*

Meanwhile, the fox-fae flew to the Abademy of Badness. It landed near the lake, where the hags were feeding the loch-monster, Vetch.

'Well, my fine foxy friend?' said Maggie Nabbie. 'How is our candidate? Has she planned her act of badness?'

'I had some doubts, but she's coming along nicely,' said the fetch, curling its tail around its paws.

'Where is she?' asked Auld Anni.

The fox-fae coughed. 'She's at Miss Kisses' Academy.'

The hags turned to stare.

'The Academy of Sweetness?' asked Kirsty. 'What's the bairn doing there?'

The fox-fae coughed again. 'I believe she's attending a pink party and practising sweet deeds.'

'That doesn't sound promising,'
said Anni.

Maggie laughed. 'Och, think o' the
mischief a bad fairy can do by trying
to be good!'

The other hags grinned.

'Exactly,' said the fox-fae. It grinned
back at the hags and zipped away.

*

Nanda was halfway to the cottage when
she realised the fox-fae wasn't with her.

That made her feel lonely, but she
tossed her head. Who needed the fetch
for company? It thought she was a *bad
fairy*! It wanted her to get a Badge of
Badness and attend a stupid Abademy!
She put it out of her mind.

'My own little cottage!' she sang, as
she reached Catkin Cottage. 'I'll keep
house! I'll do sweet deeds! I'll earn a

place at the Academy straight away!'

'What's going on?' The fox-fae popped up beside her.

'*There* you are, Foxglove.'

The fox-fae snarled. '*Don't* call me Foxglove! Are you doing a bad deed?'

'Of course not! I'm keeping house while Willow spends two days at the Fairy Floral Fair.' Nanda reached for the cottage door latch but the handle disappeared. 'I use the wand to get in,' she remembered. She waved Willow's wand. 'Open!'

The door scorched, but stayed shut. And every window was closed.

'Try gnome magic,' suggested the fox-fae.

'Foxglove, I've *told* you, I'm a fairy princess. I don't do gnome spells!'

'I said, don't call me Foxglove!' snapped the fetch.

Nanda tried the wand again.

'Oh, rockrats!' she said.★

She waggled the wand, pouring out pink sparkles. Under her breath, she whispered a gnome metal-spell. The latch popped open. With the fox-fae, Nanda stepped inside.

'It's *wonderful*,' she gloated. 'I'll do such sweet deeds here.' She skipped into Willow's bedroom.

Curious, the fox-fae followed. The wardrobe was open, revealing dainty fairy frocks.

Nanda removed her skirt and kicked it under the bed. She slipped on Willow's fanciest frock. Her wings fitted the fairy-wing slots, but she had to leave three pink pearl buttons undone.

★*Rockrats are pests that sneak about in dibbles.*

Nanda held up Willow's wand. *Flick!*
Pink sparkles flew from the tip. She
pranced around the room. The smell
of burnt sugar was everywhere.

Breathless, Nanda opened a drawer by
Willow's silken bed. She read Willow's
report from Miss Kisses' Academy.
Then she picked up a book called *Willow
Gracecloud's Book of Sweet Deeds.*

'When I go to the Academy, I'll win my Seal of Sweetness right away. I'll sit on a throne in the Pink Pavilion,' Nanda said.

'How sweet,' said the fox-fae. It leapt onto Willow's bed.

Nanda studied Willow's Sweet Deed Book. She found fairy bread in Willow's pantry, and feasted on it. The fox-fae ate some too.

'Tasteless pap,' it said, spluttering crumbs. It went off to hunt for bugs.

Secretly, Nanda agreed, but she pretended to love the sweet, bland taste.

Later, she changed into Willow's bluebird pyjamas, and climbed into Willow's bed. 'Goodnight, dear Willow,' she said, and slept.

7. Strawberries

At dawn, bluebirds sang outside the cottage. Nanda pulled the pillow over her head. 'Be quiet!' she shouted. Then she remembered. She was staying at Catkin Cottage and practising sweet deeds!

Nanda smiled, and got out of bed. Yesterday's fancy fairy frock was scorched from the wand, so she took another from the wardrobe and squeezed into it.

The fox-fae snoozed in Willow's chair. 'Good morning, dear Foxglove!' said Nanda, poking it awake.

The fetch opened beady eyes and glared. '*Don't* call me Foxglove!'

'You *are* cross,' said Nanda, 'but I forgive you.' She consulted the Sweet Deed Book. Good fairies were dainty and neat. She swept and dusted, and scarcely broke anything as she cleaned. She rehearsed Willow's lists of sweet words. 'Sweet, cute, pretty, fluffy, itsy-bitsy, inkle-winky,' she trilled.

Then her tummy rumbled loudly.

'Good fairies love baking,' said the fox-fae slyly. 'There are recipe books on the kitchen shelf.'

Nanda went to the shelf and took one down. '*Sweet Treats for Little Fairies*,' she read. '*Apple-fluff, berry tartlets, candy-coin cake . . .'* She found ingredients in the pantry, and began baking.

Soon, the kitchen smelled of hot sugar, rosewater and soot. Nanda sang sweet songs as she stirred and sifted. She used all Willow's sugar and flour. She emptied baskets and bowls and bags of ingredients. Pastries and pies steamed on the window-sill, and the fox-fae harvested samples.

'Too sweet, too burnt, and too lumpy,' it said, spluttering crumbs. 'Who's going to eat all this?'

'Me,' said Nanda.

'Fine,' said the fetch. 'Willow wouldn't want you to go hungry.' It looked happily about the messy kitchen, then went back to sleep.

Nanda wiped her greasy fingers on Willow's second-best frock. 'I'll do some more sweet deeds,' she said.

She pored over Willow's Sweet Deed Book. '*Sweet deeds are usually done for humans,*' she read. '*The sweetest deed a good fairy can do is to make a little human's wish come true.*' Nanda smiled, sweetly. 'Foxglove, I know what to do for my deed!'

'Your original bad deed?' said the fox-fae, waking up. 'It's about time!' Then its ears swivelled back against its head. '*Don't* call me Foxglove!'

Nanda sighed. 'Can't you understand? I'm a *good* fairy. I do sweet deeds. And now I know the very thing. I'm going to make a little human's wish come true. But where can I find a human?'

'There's a human village near the Academy,' said the fetch. 'I've seen one picking berries in Strawberry Meadow.'

'Perfect!' said Nanda. 'Let's go.'

'You'd better use the looking-glass
first,' said the fetch.

Nanda glanced at her reflection and
gave a squawk of dismay. 'Oh, Foxglove!
My frock is dirty, and my hair is tangled
and messy.'

'Put on another dress,' said the fox-fae.
'And *don't* call me Foxglove!'

Nanda changed into a yellow robe.

It was a pretty robe, decorated with daffodils. She tried on some silken slippers, but they were too tight. Nanda cut out the heels so she could slip them on. Then she packed fairy cakes and berry tartlets in a dainty basket, picked up Willow's wand, and set off for Strawberry Meadow.

The fox-fae buzzed gleefully after her.

Strawberry Meadow lay beyond the forest, not far from the Academy of Sweetness. Birds pecked at the wild strawberries among the grasses.

'Scat!' Nanda waved the wand.

Pink sparkles sizzled, making dark spots on the ground. The birds squawked in fright and flew off. Nanda picked a strawberry, and stuffed it into her mouth. It tasted fresh and delicious after all the sickly cakes she had eaten.

Nanda dumped her basket and Willow's wand, squatted in the grass and began gathering strawberries.

The fox-fae chased bumble bees, then settled beside Nanda. It nibbled some strawberries, but mostly, it watched Nanda eat. She moved steadily around the strawberry patch, removing ripe berries from each plant as she went. Soon Willow's daffodil robe was blotched with red strawberry juice.

Nanda popped the final ripe berry into her mouth. She chewed, swallowed, and licked her lips. 'Yum!' She sucked her fingers, then undid a few buttons.

'That's today's strawberries taken care of,' said the fox-fae, spitting out a stray hull. 'The little human will be disappointed.'

'What human?'

'The one coming to pick strawberries,' said the fetch. It flicked its tail towards a small figure plodding through the meadow.

Nanda froze. 'But I've eaten them all!' She reached for the wand.

'If you use that, you'll scorch the plants,' said the fox-fae.

Nanda's lip quivered. 'I came here to do a sweet deed, but I've spoiled everything! What will the little human think of me?'

The fetch stretched, waving its tail. 'She won't know you ate the strawberries. She won't even know you're here. Have you forgotten your DNM spell?'*

Nanda knew the fox-fae was right.

---

*Fairy breed use special 'Don't Notice Me' spells to stop humans noticing them. They are called 'DNM's for short.

While she wore her DNM no human would see or hear her. Of course, that was how good fairies made their sweet deeds into surprises. A surprise was a sweet idea, but wouldn't it be nicer if the human could thank the fairy?

Nanda made up her mind. She would follow the human until she made a wish. Then she would make it come true.

8. Eva Beleeva

Eva Beleeva was lonely. The other children in Ms Fegmeyer's class had big families. All Eva had was a sensible, busy aunt. Auntie Bess was always tidy. Her buttons matched their buttonholes, and she always knew where she was going. She wanted Eva to be busy and sensible too.

'You don't need those,' she said when

Eva asked for shoes with orange laces.

'You don't want that,' she said, when Eva asked for a necklace.

'Wait for the DVD,' she said, when Eva wanted to see Dulcinea Sweet's new film at the cinema. 'Do something useful.'

So Eva came picking strawberries. She reached the patch where the best ones grew, but today they were hard and green. Eva's eyes clouded with disappointment.

'Some greedy piggy has taken the lot,' she muttered. 'I wish I knew who it was.'

'I can grant your wish, little human,' said a voice.

Eva jumped. She had been alone in Strawberry Meadow, but suddenly someone was beside her. It looked like a sturdy little girl wearing a yellow dress that came to her ankles. The dress was stained and tight, but it was very pretty.

The girl had butter-coloured curls,
a turned-up nose and pointy ears. She'd
fastened wings to her shoulders, and she
smelled like pink bubblebath.

'Are you a pretend angel?' asked Eva.

The girl waved a pink wand. 'I am a
good fairy, here to grant your wish.'

Eva giggled. 'I bet you saw Dulcinea
Sweet's new fairy film.'

'Did you hear, little human?' asked the
girl. 'I'm about to grant your wish.'

'Go on, then,' said Eva. 'I wish——'

'You wished to know who picked the
ripe strawberries,' said the girl.

Eva remembered it was only a game.
'Tell me, then.'

The strange girl danced in a circle,
waving the pink wand. Sparks spat from
it, singeing the grass. Eva backed away.

'Your wish is *granted*!' shouted the girl.

She turned to Eva. 'A gnome ate the strawberries,' she said. 'She was very hungry, and a bad imp made her do it.'

'Gnomes? Imps?' Eva giggled. 'That's a cool wand. Where did you get it?'

'All good fairies have wands. See?' She held it out.

Eva took it carefully. The pink stick had a star at the end. She turned the wand over. It had writing along the side.

'*Willow's Wand,*' she read. 'Is your name Willow?'

The girl beamed, showing big white teeth. Her ears waggled, and the wings on her back twitched. 'No,' she said. 'I am the good fairy, Princess Alexandrite.'

'You're funny,' said Eva. 'But why did you dress up to come here?' She put out her hands to touch the girl's wings.

'Are they plastic? Or——' She broke off
as the wings moved in her hands.

The girl frowned. 'I granted your
wish. Aren't you pleased?'

'That was just a silly story,' said Eva.

The girl pouted and stamped her foot.
Eva saw her slippers were missing their
heels. 'Make another wish.'

'Um . . . what should I wish for?'

'What about a pretty necklace?'
suggested the strange girl.

'Oh yes! I wish I had a fairy necklace.'

'That's easy.' The girl wagged the wand, shooting more burnt-sugar sparks. Then she turned her back, bent down and fumbled about in the grass.

'Your wish is granted!' she said, as she dropped a necklace into Eva's hand. Eva stared in disbelief. The necklace was made of silver and shining pink stones. Then she stared at the girl, who was hopping about in circles, fluttering her wings. And *then* she realised the broken slippers were skimming the tops of the strawberry plants. The girl was flying.

'Oh, Princess Alexandrite!' gasped Eva. 'You really *are* a good fairy!'

The flying girl landed with a thud. 'Told you so.' She looked smug. 'And now I've granted a little human's dearest wish, and done the sweetest deed of all!'

9. What Good Fairies Do

After Eva Beleeva left, clutching her treasure, Nanda snatched up the fetch and kissed its snout. 'You see what a good fairy I am? I granted the little human's wish. That was a really sweet deed.'

The fox-fae grinned. 'Wasn't it lucky she wanted a necklace? Gnomes are good at making jewellery.'

'I used *fairy* magic,' said Nanda.

'Hmmm,' said the fetch. 'Let's go back to the cottage.'

Nanda spent the rest of that day practising with Willow's wand and a spellbook. Catkin Cottage smelled as if a million jam pans had boiled dry. 'I'm going to do more wishes for little humans,' she told the fox-fae. 'Miss Kisses will be delighted.' She beamed. 'I can't wait to get my pink fairy-frock uniform.'

'Change that yellow frock you're wearing now,' said the fetch. 'It needs a wash.'

Nanda pulled off the daffodil robe. She filled Willow's biggest pan with water and set it on the stove. She dumped the robe in the water and went to choose another one.

'I'll find more humans tomorrow,' she told the fox-fae.

*

Nanda meant to go straight to the human village next morning, but her tummy rumbled and somehow she found herself in Strawberry Meadow again. She was glad to see some more strawberries had ripened overnight.

'I'll taste some,' she said, 'just to be sure they're properly ripe. Making sure little humans don't get tummy aches is a sweet deed.' She picked a handful of berries. Then she moved on for more.

'Were they properly ripe?' asked the fox-fae a few minutes later.

Nanda looked sheepishly about the meadow. All the ripe strawberries were gone. Then she brightened. 'Someone's coming!'

'It's Eva Beleeva again,' said the fetch. Nanda stayed where she was as Eva

scuttled into the meadow. 'Princess
Alexandrite? I wish you'd answer me.'

Nanda took off her DNM spell.
'Your wish is granted,' she said.

Eva sighed. 'I did it again, didn't I?
I made a silly wish without thinking.
And it looks as if the naughty gnome has
stolen the strawberries again.' She smiled
at Nanda. 'Princess Alexandrite, I know
you grant wishes. What else do you do?'

'Good fairies like me bake, and grow flowers. They go to parties and do sweet deeds,' Nanda said. 'Why don't you come with me to Catkin Cottage? You can try on my frocks, and eat yummy fairy cakes.'

'Really?' squeaked Eva. 'What about Auntie Bess?'

'Why should your aunt care where you are?' asked Nanda. She grabbed Eva's hand and led her back towards the forest. As she went, she told Eva made-up stories, all about life as a good fairy. The girl listened respectfully.

Nanda decided Eva should be her new bestie. Of course she still loved Willow, but Willow was so *good*, so beautiful and so clever. Alongside Eva, Nanda was the beautiful, good and clever one.

10. Wishes and Promises

Nanda had to remove the DNM spell from Willow's cottage before she could share the cottage with Eva. She waved the wand, but the DNM remained in place. 'Rockrats!' said Nanda. She bent to touch the foundation stone.★

★*A foundation stone is the first stone laid when a building is being made. Gnome magic makes the building strong.*

'Appear!' she said, waving the wand with her other hand.

Eva yelped with delight as Catkin Cottage shifted into focus. 'Your cottage is *so* cute, Princess Alexandrite!'

'You can stay for as long as you like,' said Nanda, leading the way inside.

Eva looked about in surprise. Outside, Catkin Cottage was neat and pretty. Inside, it was a dreadful mess. Someone had been baking, and it smelled of burnt sugar. There were sticky drips on the cupboards and puddles on the floor. Towels, curtains and aprons all looked stained and greasy. Burnt pies covered every windowsill. On the stove simmered a mass of what looked like yellow dishrags.

Nanda saw her guest's expression. 'That naughty gnome came in while I was gone. Now, what shall we do first?'

Eva wanted to play dress-up, so they tried on the rest of Willow's frocks. Nanda taught Eva some fairy dances, which she made up as she went along.

'Let's have tea,' she said when she ran out of ideas. 'Foxglove, have some cakes.'

'I still have a bellyache from the last lot,' said the fox-fae. 'And *don't* call me Foxglove!' It slipped out to hunt bugs.

Nanda put Willow's best china on the table. She went to the well to fetch sugar-sip. The bluebirds squawked at her.

'I'll feed you later,' she said. 'I have a guest.'

'*Chut!*' said the bluebirds, and flew to the Academy to ask Miss Kisses for food.

Eva seemed to like the fairy cakes, though she did scrape off the burnt bits, so Nanda gave her lots of them. 'I can easily bake you some more,' she said.

'Now, do you need me to grant any wishes?'

Eva put down a half-eaten candy-coin cake. 'I wish I was special, like you,' she said.

Nanda beamed. 'Good fairies are born special. If we do sweet deeds, we get a Seal of Sweetness from dear Miss Kisses.' She told Eva about the Academy. 'We wear frilly fairy frocks with cross-stitch kisses on them. We sleep in little pink beds,

and write in our Sweet Deed Books.'

'I wished *I* was special, Eva' reminded Nanda. 'Can't you grant my wish?'

Nanda had no idea how to make Eva special, but she smiled. 'Good fairies can do anything. But you must be ready.'

'I wish *I* was a good fairy,' said Eva. Then she giggled. 'But then, I wouldn't need you to grant my wishes. I'd grant wishes myself!'

'Why not?' said Nanda. 'If you become a good fairy like me, you could live in Catkin Cottage. And you could come to the Academy of Sweetness. You'd love it there, Eva. The fairies have such a sweet time.' She waved her wand at Eva. Sparks shot out and Eva ducked.

'Your wish is granted!' said Nanda.

Eva's eyes widened. 'Am I a real fairy now?' she asked.

'You're a brand new good fairy,' said Nanda. She felt smug. Making Eva happy was a very sweet deed. Eva didn't have to know it was all pretend.★

Eva put her hand on her tummy. 'I feel a bit sick.'

'The human's had too much fairy cake and sugar-sip,' said the fox-fae. It had sneaked back into the cottage and was cleaning its toes in Willow's best chair.

Nanda frowned at the fetch. 'Don't be silly, Foxglove, dear.'

'Don't call me Foxglove!' snapped the fox-fae.

Nanda ignored that. 'It's all right, Eva,' she said. 'Brand new fairies have to get used to being special instead of ordinary.'

★*Fairies know it is impossible for humans to be anything but humans.*

'She's green,' said the fox-fae. 'Maybe you turned her into a pixie by mistake.'

'Now I'm a fairy, I want to fly,' said Eva. She put her hand up onto her shoulder. 'Where are my wings?'

'They take a while to grow,' said Nanda. 'It's like strawberries. One day there aren't any, then there are little green ones. Then they get bigger.'

Eva sighed. 'I have a tummy ache, Princess Alexandrite. I wish I——'

'Let's play princesses again,' said Nanda.

'I have to lie down,' said Eva.

Nanda led Eva to Willow's room. Crumpled frocks covered the bed, so Nanda dumped them on the floor. Eva lay down with a moan.

Back in the kitchen, Nanda pouted. It had been fun playing with Eva, but it wasn't fun any more.

'I could have told you this would happen,' said the fox-fae.

'Why didn't you?'

'I'm a bad fairy,' said the fetch. 'Why should I care if a greedy human gets stomach-ache?' It grinned. 'Oh, I forgot. She's not human. Princess Alexandrite turned her into a brand new good fairy. No, wait . . . Nanda the naughty gnome *pretended* to turn her into a fairy.'

'I had to pretend to grant her wish,' said Nanda. 'Otherwise, she would have been disappointed. Good fairies don't disappoint little humans.'

While Eva slept off the effects of too much fairy cake and sugar-sip, Nanda played at princesses. She admired herself in the looking-glass and invented more fairy dances. She thought about baking, but all the trays and basins were burnt and sticky. There were no more frocks to try on, and the spellbook had fallen in a puddle of unset toffee.

A smell of burning made her hurry to the stove. The daffodil robe had been simmering, but the water had boiled away and now the robe was blackened and burnt.

'Oh, *rockrats!*' complained Nanda, fanning smoke away. 'I'll never get into the Academy at this rate.' She sighed. 'I wish Eva would wake up.'

The fox-fae went to check on the sleeping girl. 'Still green,' it said. 'Try fresh air.'

Nanda bounced onto the bed, almost knocking Eva to the floor. 'Wake up!' she said. 'We're going out to enjoy the lovely sunshine!'

11. Weeping Willow

Willow had enjoyed the Fairy Floral Fair, but she was looking forward to going home to her own sweet cottage. She hoped Nanda was having a lovely time.

It would be a very sweet deed if an ordinary gnome learned to be a good fairy. Willow smiled as she left the fair and flew eagerly towards the forest.

And there it was! Dear, dear Catkin

Cottage! 'I'm home!' trilled Willow. She twirled in the air, and landed on tiptoe. 'Bluebirds, dear bluebirds! I'm home! Sweet flowers, I'm home!' She held out her arms for the bluebirds to land on.

But where were they? It was so quiet. And what *was* that horrible smell?

Willow stared around. The cottage door was open and *someone had taken off the cottage's DNM spell*!

Willow turned her mouth up in a sweet smile. 'Nanda's just left the door open,' she said aloud. 'She took off the cottage's DNM to welcome me!'

'You think?' said a sharp voice. Willow blinked as the fox-imp that followed Nanda everywhere zipped over her shoulder to hover by her nose. 'Think again,' said the fox-fae. It cackled, and flew away, its tail streaming behind it.

Willow entered the cottage.

The smell of burning made her eyes water so she had to blink away tears. She rubbed her eyes and stared at the mess of ruined food. Could this be her dear cottage? It should be neat and sweet! It should smell of flowers and pink sugar! Willow's lips trembled, and, for the first time ever, she wept.

That *poor* little gnome! She must have tried *so* hard to make a welcome-home feast for Willow!

'I'll tell Miss Kisses!' said Willow aloud. 'Little Nanda has to go to the Academy and learn to do sweet deeds properly.' She cast a clean-up spell, then flew away.★

*

'How do you feel?' asked Nanda, as she and Eva skipped through the forest.

'A little better,' said Eva bravely. She looked towards the slanting sun. 'I should go home to Auntie Bess.'

'No hurry,' said Nanda. 'Remember, you're a fairy now.'

Eva sighed. 'I can't wait to feel special.

★*Most fairies do housework by hand, because that's a sweet deed. If they're in a hurry, they use magic.*

When will that part of the wish come true?'

'Soon,' said Nanda. 'First, you need a magic wand. There's one over there!' She pointed to a long twig.

Eva picked it up. 'Can we tidy the cottage? That naughty gnome made such a mess.'

'Of course!' said Nanda. 'Good fairies love cleaning. As a special treat, I'll let you do it all! It will be your very first sweet deed!'

But when they arrived at the cottage, it was already clean.

'It's magic!' cried Eva. 'Did the cottage clean itself?'

'Well . . . um . . .' For the first time, Nanda stumbled for a reply. Dibbles and cribs didn't clean themselves, but what about fairy cottages? She noticed that the fox-fae was curled on Willow's favourite chair. 'Foxglove will explain,' she said. 'I'll make syrup crinkles for supper.' She began to rattle pans.

'But——' Eva broke off. 'Is that someone calling my name?'

12. An Auntie Arrives

'Don't be silly,' said Nanda. 'Who'd be calling for *you*? Here!' She snatched up the stick she had found in the forest. 'Practise spells with your new wand.'

'I'm sure I can hear someone,' insisted Eva.

The fox-fae flew out to investigate.

'It's a human,' it reported, when it returned.

'*Oooh!* Now I'm a good fairy, I can grant a wish!' said Eva. 'Princess Alexandrite, show me——'

'You're not ready to grant wishes yet.' Nanda stirred the sugary mess in the pan.

'I have to start sometime,' said Eva. She fluffed up the skirts of the frilly fairy frock she had borrowed from Willow's cupboard. Then she raised the wand, and stepped outside. The fox-fae followed.

'Eva, *Ev-a*!' The person hurrying through the twilight towards Catkin Cottage couldn't be her aunt. Auntie Bess was neat, tidy and sensible. *This* person's bun was falling down, and her blouse was torn.

'*Eva!*'

'Auntie Bess?' Eva darted through the garden and into the forest. 'What's wrong?'

'Oh, *Eva*! How can you ask that? You've been gone all day! I thought you were lost.'

'I'm fine,' said Eva. Her voice was muffled as her aunt hugged her. 'Oh, Auntie Bess, I met a real live fairy princess, and she turned *me* into a fairy too. Now I can be special.'

Auntie Bess dabbed her eyes then quickly tidied her bun. 'What do you mean, special?'

'Um . . .' Eva was taken by surprise. 'Important and interesting?' she suggested.

'You don't have to be a fairy to be important and interesting,' said Auntie Bess, frowning. 'You are important by being *yourself* and thinking for yourself. And you can be interesting by being interested. Do you understand?'

'But I don't feel special,' said Eva.

'Well, you are special and you should feel it,' said Auntie Bess. 'I see we have important things to talk about.'

Eva took her aunt's hand. Then suddenly she pulled away and ran back through the dusk to the cottage.

Nanda turned to meet her. 'Ready for supper?'

'No thanks,' said Eva. 'I've changed my mind. I don't want to be a fairy.'

'Of course you do!' burst out Nanda. 'You want to be special, don't you?'

'Auntie Bess says I'm special because I'm *me*,' said Eva. 'And being a good fairy *isn't* being me. So I'm going home.' She removed the pink fairy frock and ran off in her shorts and shirt, leaving Nanda alone.

Nanda sat on the cottage step, and tried to think of a sweet deed. She could find another little human to help, or feed carrots to some bunnies. She thought of lots of things, but then she realised that she didn't really feel like doing sweet deeds. 'Foxglove!' she called. 'Supper time!'

The fox-fae didn't answer.

Nanda bit into a syrup crinkle, but it tasted far too sweet for her to finish.

'I'll give it to the bluebirds,' she said aloud. She took the plate down the garden to the cotes where the bluebirds lived.*

'Suppertime, bluebirds!' she called, but the cotes were empty.

Nanda's lips quivered as she returned to the cottage. 'It's not fair!' she said. 'I'm a *good* fairy, but everyone's left me. Eva's gone. After all I did for her! The bluebirds have gone. Foxglove's deserted me.' She sniffled. 'Eva's auntie came looking for her, but no one ever looks for *me*. And I minded the cottage *so* well.' A fat tear plopped on the frothy fairy frock as she stepped inside. The cottage was so clean and pretty . . . apart from the messy kitchen. Nanda headed that way.

Cotes are fancy little bird houses.

She didn't want syrup crinkles, but maybe she could roast an egg or something.

She took an egg from a pink china bowl, and thought sadly of the sweet deeds she had done that day. Eva hadn't been a bit grateful. Just a bit green.

Although Eva had looked awfully funny when she felt for wings that would never grow. And the fox-fae had looked funny when it snarled at her for calling it Foxglove. And Willow . . . Nanda thought how funny Willow would look when she came home and found a new mess in her kitchen. She'd *try* to look sweet, but would she manage?

Nanda giggled.

13. Academy? Abademy?

Nanda was woken next morning by a sharp rapping on the front door.

'Go away!' she shouted.

The rapping stopped. Then came pinging sounds as the hinges popped off the door. Sturdy footsteps followed.

'Just as I thought!' said a voice.

Nanda's eyes popped open and she looked up at two familiar gnome faces.

She smiled. 'Hello Gramma Glim! Hello Grandpa Clog!'

'Nanda Gemdibbler, I told you to come *straight home!*' scolded Gramma.

Nanda sat up. 'But I've been helping Willow.'

The old gnomes exchanged glances. 'Look, Princess,' said Grandpa. 'We want you to be helpful, but ... well ...' His voice trailed off.

'We want you to be helpful like a gnome!' said Gramma. 'Gnomes work hard in dibbles and cribs. They *don't* gad about pretending to be good fairies.'

'We were worried about you,' said Grandpa.

Nanda got up, dressed, and hugged them. 'There's no need to worry about me, ever again,' she said, giving each a smacking kiss on the cheek.

'I've learned *lots* by doing sweet deeds, and now I know where I belong.'

'So do we!' chimed in a new voice from the kitchen.

'Miss Kisses!' whooped Nanda, and scooted out of Willow's bedroom, fluttering her wings madly. 'Miss Kisses! Willow!' She flung herself at the startled fairies, and sneezed.

'Hello Nanda!' said Willow faintly. She glanced at the new mess in the kitchen.

Miss Kisses held up a notebook, covered with pink stars. 'I've been looking in my Fairy-Reporter, and guess what I found?'*

'Trouble, if it's about our Nanda,' said Gramma Glim, folding her arms.

---

*A Fairy-Reporter is a magical book that helps good-fairy teachers keep track of their pupils.

'No!' cooed Miss Kisses. '*This* little gnome has been doing sweet deeds!'

'Right,' agreed Nanda. 'I looked after Willow's cottage, and baked sweet treats.'

'But your *big* sweet deed was making a little human feel special!' interrupted Miss Kisses. 'You showed Eva Beleeva how to be special, and now her auntie can see it too. And it's all because a dear little gnome worked hard at being sweet.'

'*Oooh!*' said Nanda. She looked towards the stove. 'I must bake some sweet treats for *you*, Miss Kisses.'

'I'll do that,' said Willow quickly. 'Miss Kisses has something for you, Nanda.'

'Is it sugar-sip?' asked Nanda.

'Can't you guess?' Miss Kisses offered Nanda a fat pink brooch.

'*Ooh!*' Nanda clasped her hands together. 'My very own Seal of Sweetness!'

'Yes!' said Miss Kisses. 'Your very own Seal of Sweetness, because you proved, once and for all, that a gnome can become a good fairy.'

'So you'll go to the Academy of Sweetness right away,' put in Willow.

Nanda beamed. 'It's *sooo* sweet to know where I belong at last.' Then, overcome by the powerful smell of pink bubblegum, she sneezed.

'What have we here?' asked yet another voice.

Miss Kisses drew her skirts aside as three water hags, accompanied by the fox-fae, peered through the open door. 'Good morning Kirsty,' she said. 'I see you found some—um—friends.'

'Aye,' said Kirsty Breeks.* She turned to Maggie Nabbie. 'So, this is the wee gnome candidate,' she remarked.

'It is,' said Maggie. She nodded to Grandpa Clog and Gramma Glim. 'Are you ready to let wee Nanda be herself?'

'I suppose so,' said Gramma. 'If it makes her happy.'

Nanda sneezed again at the pink bubblegum scent of Miss Kisses' robes. 'Hello Foxglove!' she said, swooping to kiss the fox-fae. 'Guess what! Miss Kisses gave me a Seal of Sweetness!' She grinned as the fetch bared its teeth. 'She invited me to the Academy.'

'So that's it, is it?' said the fox-fae. 'After all my hard work, you're still set on going to that awful old pink place.'

---

*Kirsty Breeks used to work at the Academy as a cleaner.

It snuffled and rubbed at its snout with one paw. 'Don't expect me to visit you. The smell of sweet deeds makes me sneeze.'

Nanda looked at her Seal of Sweetness. It was pink, and very shiny. It smelled powerfully of pink bubblegum. She smiled at Miss Kisses and Willow. 'Thank you *so* much for giving me this,' she said. 'It was *so* sweet of you, and I'll always be grateful, but . . . *a-a-choo*!' She sneezed. Then she sighed and held out the Seal to Miss Kisses. 'I'm afraid I can't accept it.'

'But Nanda dear, you deserve it!' said Miss Kisses. She felt among her skirts and fished out a wand. 'See? I even have a brand new wand for you!'

Nanda took the wand and waved it. Sparks shot out, leaving little smoking holes in Miss Kisses' gown and filling the room with the smell of burnt sugar.

Nanda sniffed the smell with pleasure.
'I've realised I'm not cut out to be a good
fairy after all,' she said. 'I can see now
that I'm like Foxglove. The smell of pink
bubblegum makes me sneeze. I think
I'm allergic to it.' She put down the
wand and turned to the hags. 'But after
all my sweet deeds, am I bad enough for
your Abademy?'

Maggie smiled. '*Which* sweet deeds?

Apart from accidentally helping Eva and her aunt?' Maggie ticked off deeds on her fingers. 'You pretended to be sweet. That was bad. You lied to that human, and that was bad too. You made fairy wands shoot out sparks of burnt sugar which is just plain naughty. And for a breath-taking act of badness, you let Willow Gracecloud and Miss Kisses waste a good deal of sweetness on you. They could have used it on someone who deserved it instead.' She paused. 'What do you say to that, Nanda Gemdibbler?'

Nanda pouted, then grinned. 'Um . . .'

'Wait,' said Gramma Glim. She turned to the hags. 'I don't pretend Nanda is a perfect gnome,' she said, 'but she tried to be good.'

'Good or not,' said Grandpa Clog, 'she'll always be our princess.'

'It's all right, Gramma and Grandpa,' said Nanda. 'I am what I am, and now I *know* what I am.' She turned back to Maggie. 'What do I say to that? I ruined Willow's dresses. I cut up her slippers. I wasted her flour. I drove away the bluebirds, and made a mess of Catkin Cottage.' She considered for a moment, then continued. 'I broke a bed at the Academy, and flooded the pink bathroom. I worried my grandparents. I *pretended* to be sweet, but I see now I was reckless, selfish, mendaciously misleading, very vain and mindbogglingly bad. Maybe you should give me that Badge of Badness right away!'

A Note from Tiffany Mandrake

Psst, this is me, Tiffany Mandrake, again.

Nanda has been at the Abademy of Badness for a year. She is still a naughty gnome, but sometimes she puts on a frilly frock, and does a sweet deed, just to annoy the fox-fae.

I live in a cosy, creepy cottage in the Abademy grounds. The hags know I'm here, and they trust me completely.

They know I'll never say a word . . . and I haven't . . .

. . . except to you.

About the Author

Bad behaviour is nothing new to Tiffany Mandrake—some of her best friends are Little Horrors! And all sorts of magical visitors come to her cosy, creepy cottage in the grounds of the Hags' Abademy.

Tiffany's favourite creature is the dragon who lives in her cupboard and heats water for her bath. She rather hopes the skunk-fae doesn't come to visit again, for obvious reasons.

About the Artist

Martin Chatterton once had a dog called Sam, who looked exactly like a cocker spaniel ... except she was much smaller and had wings. According to Martin, she even used to flutter around his head and say annoying things. Hmmm!

Martin has done so many bad deeds he is sure he deserves several Badges of Badness. 'Never trust a good person' is his motto.

Other Titles in the Series

Flax the Feral Fairy

Mal the Mischievous Mermaid

Tikki the Tricky Pixie